That Crazy Barb'ra

by Milton Schafer   illustrated by G. Brian Karas

Dial Books for Young Readers   New York

Published by Dial Books for Young Readers, A division of Penguin Young Readers Group, 345 Hudson Street, New York, New York 10014, Text copyright © 2003 by Milton Schafer, Illustrations copyright © 2003 by G. Brian Karas, All rights reserved, Manufactured in China on acid-free paper, Library of Congress Cataloging-in-Publication Data, Schafer, Milton. That crazy Barb'ra / by Milton Schafer ; illustrations by G. Brian Karas. p. cm. Summary: Hubert Clumpty says he wishes his classmate "crazy Barb'ra" would leave him alone. ISBN 0-8037-2584-1 [1. Interpersonal relations—Fiction. 2. Stories in rhyme.] I. Karas, G. Brian, ill. II. Title. PZ8.3.S2893 Th 2003 [E]—dc21 2001007348

10 9 8 7 6 5 4 3 2 1

The art was created using gouache, acrylics, and pencil.
The text was hand-lettered by the artist.

For Frank Loesser and Donna Rubin,
with love—for their energy,
support, and inspiration
—M.S.

For Judy
—G.B.K.

oh!

That crazy Barb'ra!
Boy, is she a pest!

In school she leans
all over me

And copies
off my test.

She's got the desk
behind me,
She pokes me with
her toes.

And every time I turn around,
She wrinkles up her nose.

And yesterday practically in front of the Whole class She goes and blurts out:

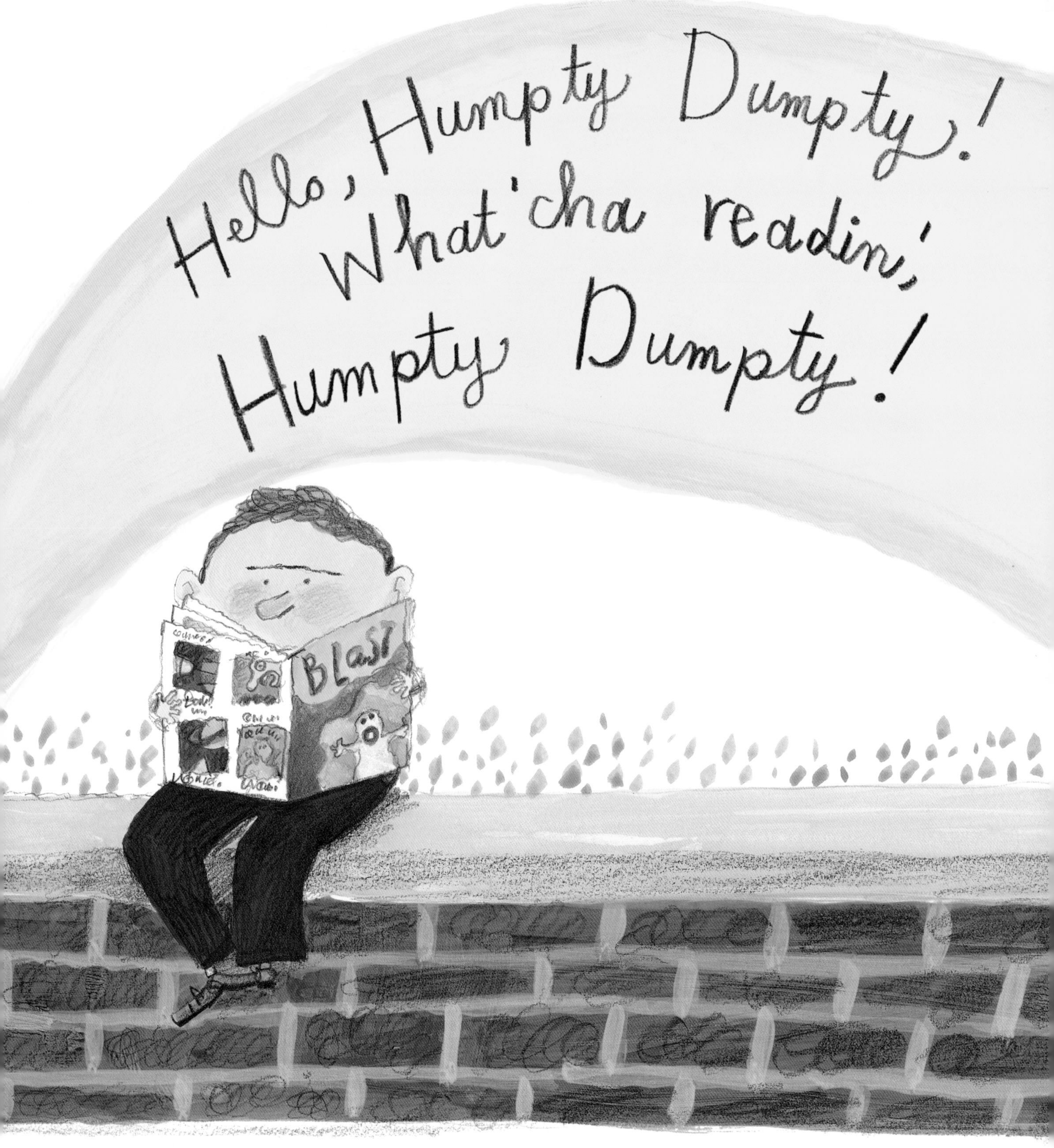
Hello, Humpty Dumpty!
What'cha readin',
Humpty Dumpty!
BLAST

And everyone knows
she's talkin' about ME—

'coz my name
is Hubert Clumpty!

Ooh, that crazy Barb'ra,
Always askin' where I've been.

I wish that she'd butt out
for once

Instead of buttin' in.

Once when I went
swimmin'
And I had nothin'
on,
I looked back toward
the shore

and all my clothes were gone!

At first I thought it must be Artie,
Actin' like a big fat Smarty.

But then I heard
this voice
Yellin' down at me:

That crazy, crazy Barb'ra
Was hangin' from a tree!

Boy, one of

these days. <u>Just</u> one of these days...

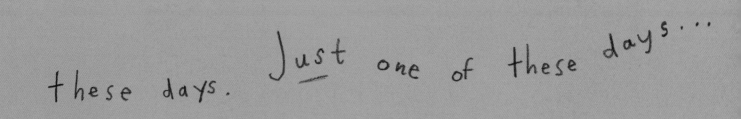

Barb'ra has
to be on my
team,
But she
can't play
at all!

And every time

She misses

She's up at bat,
every ball!

So what if Alvin Schmauder
Likes her looks and makes a
fuss.

You'll never ever catch me
Sittin' with her on
the bus.

I wish I didn't have to be
Her husband in the play
'Coz when I have to kiss her,
All the guys'll say:

"Hum-Dum loves Barb'ra!
Hum-Dum loves
Hum-Dum loves
Barb'ra!"
AND I DON'T!

Ooh, that crazy Barb'ra! Can't stand that crazy Barb'ra! And I'll never marry her...

Someday.